ABHIVYAKTI

ABHIVYAKTI

STUTI AGNIHOTRI

Abhivyakti *by* Stuti Agnihotri

Published in 2018 by www.pblishing.com

Marketed by

Maple Press Private Limited
Sales Office A 63, Sector 58, Noida 201 301, U.P., India
phone +91 120 455 3581, 455 3583
email info@**maple**press.co.in
website www.**maple**press.co.in

ISBN: 978-93-87348-16-5

10 9 8 7 6 5 4 3 2 1

Dedicated to

The most sweet and stubborn lady I had ever seen - my grandmother.

Contents

Acknowledgements 9

1. Life & Cookies 13

2. My Heroes Without Capes 15

3. Sunny Side Up 17

4. Mirror 19

5. Chalks & Rain 21

6. Tiny Friend of Mine 23

7. Buch 25

8. Spring 27

9. Sun & Moon 29

10. Literature 31

11. Women 33

12. Cocoon 35

13. Fly High 37

14. Blue Clock 39

15. Teddy Bear 41

16. Ocean 43

17. Dear Smashed Flower 44

18. Childhood Calls 45

19. Colours 46

20. Antevasin 47

21. High Heels 48

22. Urban Musings 49

23. New One's Arrival...50

24. Reborn 51

25. Ardour 52

26. Carry What You Love 53

27. Wings to Fly 54

28. Elevator...55

About the Author 56

Crowd-Funders...61

ACKNOWLEDGEMENTS

First of all, I am really overwhelmed on the completion and compilation of 'Abhivyakti'.

The people who played an active role in the making of this book are as crazy as its author and deserve special thanks.

To begin with, I would like to thank my family who always promoted my desire to write and at the same time taught me how to manage my life while balancing my profession and passion.

Secondly, a big thanks to all my friends and acquaintances who unfailingly encouraged me to chase my dreams and let go of the shyness that has been an inherent part of my personality.

A special mention is due here for all my teachers, who have taught me till date, because it were you who made me realize that I had this ability to express my thoughts into words and motivated me to go further in my endeavors.

Also, a huge thanks to my publishers, for making my dream come true.

POEMS

Inspired by everyone I know till date,
I write because I love to.

COOKIES

LIFE & COOKIES

Life is like a cookie, sweet and hard.

We're gently thrown towards the earth, like how sieved flour is thrown on the platform with dreams of the most amazing journey

The moment we realize what's around, we are set free to mix with our surroundings like how the all purpose flour is allowed free to go and mix with milk

In no time we find ourselves being kneaded amidst the people like how the dough is kneaded within fingers

And when we blend well with the society we get a place of our own like how the cookies in-their-making get on the baking tray

We're heated under the daily chaos slowly and steadily like how the cookies are baked

Finally we take a dip in and a dip out of our monotonous lives which does have some beautiful halts, until we are all eaten up and done.

DAD.
ME.
MOM.

MY HEROES WITHOUT CAPES

To any problem arriving
He stands hard and tall
To any mischief done
She still loves us all
It is because of him
Our home is without troubles
It is because of her
Our home is filled with giggles
From making pizzas to pastas and bringing books and pen
They both made my life as blissful as heaven
He is my brave father, the hero of my dreams
She is my sweet mother, the angel of all queens.

Live Life

SUNNY SIDE UP

Pour strong smelling coffee from the thermos in a cup
With wide smile on the face
And the sunny side up

Leave the daily race in between and get lost into nature's lap
Think how something can be so beautiful and soothing
Can it be a trap?

Let out your worries along with carbon dioxide and inhale
happiness and fresh air
Sink in the soft mud and enjoy the green grass, the enjoyment you
never found even by sitting in the most expensive and cozy chair

Get nostalgic and gather back the fun you had when with your
friends you did play
Regret spending your whole time being deeply engrossed and lost
in that four inch display

Sink in deeper in the soft mud and release the monotony out
Listen to your soul and let your passion out

Enjoy the setting sun, and get lost in the beauty of the waned
moon
Put your sunny side up, and start living for your own self, because
you're not a toon

MIRROR MIRROR
ON THE
Wall .....

MIRROR

The girl in the mirror looks exactly like me
Even she makes weird sounds when she laughs with glee

But she raises her left hand when I raise my right
Although like me, even she has an average height

And sometimes I think whether even she over thinks upon
anything and everything like me
And longs to have a secret magical house up high on the tree

We sat in front of the mirror with a book in my hand the whole
day
And in between reading we both stared at each other without
saying either a 'hi' a 'hello' or a 'hey'

I noticed that even she smirks in between like me, while reading
the book
And at times when I felt I hated the part, she gave that same 'I
hate it too' look

I wonder whether even she would be confused while making out
what's right and what's wrong
And thinks stupid stuff instead of sleeping, all night long

I was irritated at first to find that someone had the same unibrow
like me

But I've started to like that girl inside the mirror, I see

You can find seven more people that look like you people say
Why not wait and look out for the one in the mirror one pretty
day?

CHALKS & RAIN

We throw chalks on each other's head
And eat and spill each other's food as if little babies are being fed
We hear our teachers and parents complain
And rush out to the sports ground even if its heavy rain

Dear each and every school friend
Thank you so much to give all days in the school, a happy end.

MR. SQUIRREL!

TINY FRIEND OF MINE

This thought came to my mind when I was enjoying the drizzle and smooth winds on a calm monsoon evening, with my snacks placed on my lap. I was enjoying this blissful scene, through my window, with one hand placed on the window sill, while the other hand was busy helping me eat my sandwich. My window was covered by a green colored wire so that no pigeons enter there to lay eggs. And then, squeezing itself through the intersection in the green wire, came my cute little friend. He started nibbling a part of it and pushed himself inside and caught hold of me with its mesmerizing blue eyes. I couldn't resist myself not offering him a piece of my sandwich to fill his tiny stomach. Watching him nibble the bread bit after bit was the best scene to ever witness.

There he was, probably the cutest creation of God, my friend – the squirrel. This made me go into a deep thought, which was more of a spiral thought – with no end.

What if the Almighty, at the time of making us, had asked us about what we want to be? Probably, I wouldn't have chosen to become a human being, it's just lots of exams and nothing. I would have definitely wished to become a squirrel just like the one I saw - soft and furry, with three symmetrical lines going through the back of my hazel colored body. I would have surely pleaded for those beautiful pearl like eyes as well. I would then have surely enjoyed my life to the fullest, running around on my tiny feet, nibbling nuts with my funny teeth. Like a forest officer, I would have roamed every single corner of my area, meeting birds and bugs of all kinds. I would have surely stored all my best nuts in the tree at my present aunt's garden. The best part of it would have been the elimination of school life. No mathematical algorithms, physical laws, and chemical equations would be ever revolving around my head. In fact, I would instead have loved to sit in the middle of my present school assembly area, gazing the school building all day long through my marble like eyes. I would have just solely belonged to my mother earth, enjoying the essence of lying in her lap. Thinking a bit offside, I could have become the model of some professional wildlife photographers as well! The best part of it? I could keep posing for photographs all day without them teaching me how to do that. Apart from all these things, I could have got an access to all those banished places of the world where people aren't allowed much. Be it the president's house or a small hole in the tree trunk, it would just be me who would decide what to do. I could keep leaping all day long and even turn my ankles up to 180 degrees. Getting to use my tail, to talk to my pals in a secret code language would have been the thing I would do all day long. The only thing I would have feared of would be to stop gnawing, because I know that the moment I had decided to stop that, my teeth would grow into my neck, taking away the cuteness factor of mine – the kind of asset that I would love to behold. If someone would have kept me as a pet, then I would have shown him/her the affection they wanted and become dependent on him/her for food. Honestly, I would just have enjoyed every moment of my short life. But all my beautiful imaginary memories broke up into pieces as soon as I realized that my little chum had gone.

I wish I could turn back the clock and bring the wheels of time to a stop and stay there, in the thoughts of living in between the trees forever.

BUCH

It wore a thin jacket, so sleek and perfect
I ran my fingers down its spine
And a beautiful smell came from within
It was my book, asking me to get lost into its words.

HELLO SPRING

SPRING

The leaves of winter rejoice on the snow bed
To get flown away by the heavy sighs of creatures
To get crushed beneath their paws

As spring arrives.

SUN & MOON

And when the moon started feeling that the sun was prudish
It never thought that it was the same sun that burns itself everyday
so that the moon shines.

LITERATURE

And set me free to go on the path of literature
I'll entwine myself along with the words
And sew them with a needle in the lace of beauty

Though grammar may prick me sometimes.

32

WOMEN

The most delicate creature in her making
Signed an indenture before she was sent to earth that she'll handle everything and everyone
Be it good times or bad.

A woman she is.

____

to every woman I adore, maa

BUTTERFLY
CATERPILLAR

COCOON

Wrapped as tender cocoons we took our own time to adjust and grow
But my wings as a butterfly are yet to adjust these gusty winds.

Because I am still latent and immature.

fly
HIGH

FLY HIGH

To chase your dreams that are misty,
And to polish your skills that are dusty,
Fly High!

To catch hold of what you desire,
And to get something that you admire,
Fly High!

CLOCK

BLUE CLOCK

Tick-tock Tick-tock says the blue clock staring at my face,
To hold my breath and buck up strength to be steady in the race.

Tick-tock Tick-tock says the blue clock showing me the time,
And telling me to enjoy the moment as everything is going to be fine.

MR·TEDDY

TEDDY BEAR

Dear dusty teddy bear lying on the rack,
You have a furry body and a hunchback,
In your gleaming eyes I see the memories of the day,
When I was a kid and we, did play.

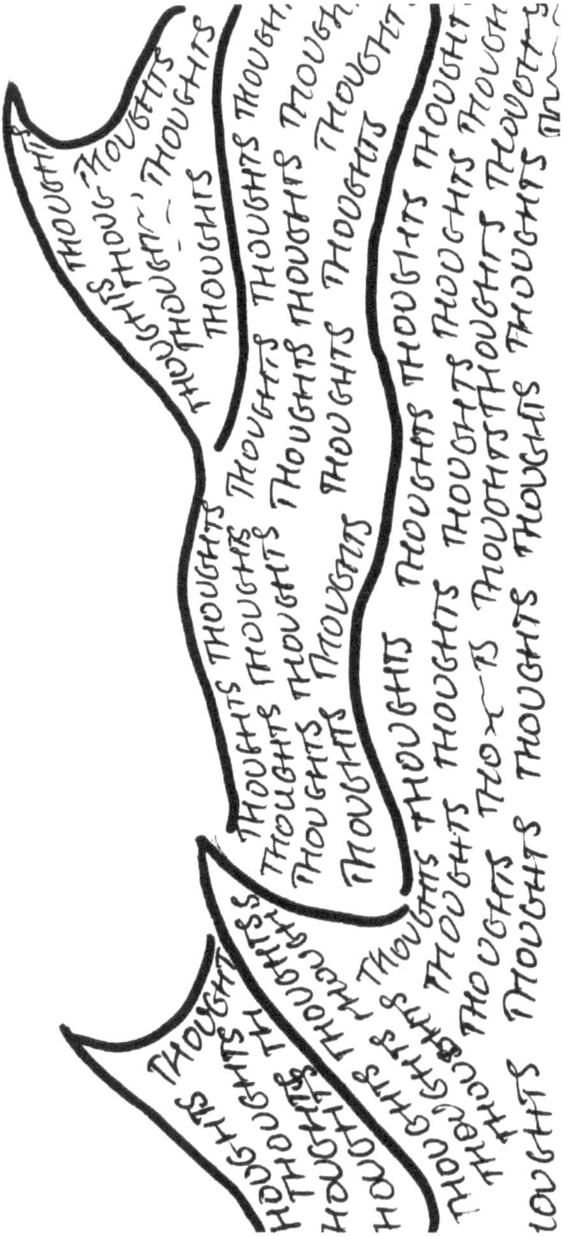

OCEAN

The waves of the ocean come and go every day.
I wish that was the same with thoughts.

DEAR SMASHED FLOWER

Dear smashed flower lying on the sidewalk,

There may be many people who crush you more, swish you aside
and ignore your presence
But then there are those souls who'll pick you up and keep you
with them

Because you're still beautiful.

CHILDHOOD CALLS

The memories of past echo with a voice like that of a child
Of the days when the dreams were aspiring and wild
Unpleasantly, the memories perish like forgotten dreams
Where the roads were made of chocolates and houses were made
of ice-creams.

COLOURS

Red poses anger
Red poses love
It isn't just a colour, but something too much.

colours carry more power than we do

ANTEVASIN

In the twenty-first century world, everyone has entangled themselves amidst money, fame and glee

And thus, in the want of peace and harmony, my inner soul makes me feel that it is an 'antevasin' I want to be.

HIGH HEELS

I forgot all my musing to own good heels and branded shoes,
The day I discovered those tiny hand-woven baby shoes hanging in my mother's bedroom
The ones that I used to wear when I was small.

URBAN MUSINGS

Life has become a roller coaster
Where everyone is running to become the best and stay alive
People have now become huge boasters
All they do is stupidly strive

Life has now become a joke
Where not caring for others has become the new trend
Instead of midnight calls and messages I now receive Facebook pokes
These are the musings of having a virtual friend

These are the perks of living in the 21st century amidst hatred, attitude and ego
I wish I was born some time back, where friends were more and less were foe

NEW ONE'S ARRIVAL

I wandered all around the house
Finding my mother just like a mouse
I couldn't find her anywhere
It was an irritation I couldn't bear
Then I saw my dad sitting on the chair
He was excited, I know, I swear
He told me softly your mother will soon come
But she'll have a baby, who'll be your chum
I was extremely happy and jumped like a fool
But to my sorrow, I had to go to school
With no thoughts about the morning, I entered the room's hall
And my father exclaimed, "It's a girl – she looks just like a delicate doll"
I was feeling like I stepped over the moon
And wanted to meet the baby very soon
My father too smiled, a bit too long and big
His smile was as sweet as a fig
In minutes he took me to her and everyone there was happy I know,
My sister's cheeks were as soft as snow.
A sparkle in everyone's eyes I could see,
And resolved from that very day 'a good sister I would be.'

REBORN

The day I chose to leave everyone flabbergasted
Leaving them amidst their jealousy and hatred
Helped me stand up hard and strong
And made me realize it wasn't me who always committed
something wrong.

The day I chose to defend unwanted travail
Boosted my self-esteem and set my sail
It taught me that it is always about self-realization
And not about public chosen manifestation.

The day I chose to not to be on my lowest low
I became my own helping hand and gave a throw
I pulled myself up, out of the pit
And that gave me a push, the candle had finally lit.

The day I chose to rejoice
I understood it all about hearing your own voice
Be it a slow–coach or an expeditious man
Life is finally about the fellow who thinks he can.

ARDOUR

My life was all bland and boring
It felt like the mansion's old wooden flooring
Apathetic, tranquil and tedious it was
It felt like my life has no cause
And then books came into my life

Non- fiction books became my motivation and dystopian my love
They fitted so perfectly in my life, the way a hand fits in a glove
A chum, a pathfinder these books became my everyday need
Even school and reference books felt like to be given a read

I had a change in my perspective
I started analyzing everything like a detective
Fictional concepts became my core
And motivational stuff molded me more
They groomed me good and soothed me well
Living amidst books is a feeling hard to expel

You call them books I call them my buch
A cuppa, my specs and them with me are always too much

CARRY WHAT YOU LOVE

Carry what you love
Be it funky tattoos, piercings or a long leather glove

Nine stitches on the hand and a scar on the face
Carry it if you love it, you're not different from the race

Wear a short skirt with yellow lip colour if it's your style
There will be people who'll love and hate you for this at every
mile

Wear long thorny jackets with black and dark hues
If they mean something to you and are your muse

Being chubby is cute and there is no bad in having a double chin
But only till the time it doesn't affect your health and tense your
kin

Be it a palazzo, a burkha or a saree with a blouse
Admiring yourself in front of the mirror is okay, but not judging
your own self without stepping out of the house

Carry what you love be it a beauty mark or a mar
You look beautiful when you love yourself because no one is
perfect, neither me nor you and not even the super stars

WINGS TO FLY

And in the search for wings to fly
Do enjoy the essence of soft mud under your bare feet
Stand on your toes - a bit high
And let the fresh grass tickle you from beneath.

ELEVATOR

The elevator in my building has a long mirror inside
I make weird faces every time I am alone in it as it accelerates up

Negative Gravity, Positive Mind.

ABOUT THE AUTHOR

Date of Birth: 06 May, 2001

Place of Birth: Punjab, India

 boowaandkwala@gmail.com

https://twitter.com/theinkedweirdo

https://www.instagram.com/theinkedweirdo

https://www.goodreads.com/book/show/40498278-abhivyakti

Stuti Agnihotri is chirpy sixteen-year–old girl who is currently studying in class twelve. She is a school student by profession and a scribbler by heart but struggles to balance her schooling and passion at the same time.

Reading books on a variety of topics influenced her to such an extent that she stepped into the domain of writing. Reading a dictionary to hunt for new words is her favorite pastime and counts for her unique approach while playing with words. She ponders over every little thought that crosses her mind and tries to express her emotions through her writings.

Live Life

ABHIVYAKTI

STUTI AGNIHOTRI

Did you like the book **?**

Email your questions,
experiences, and suggestions to
the author at
boowaandkwala@gmail.com

CROWD-FUNDERS

(names listed alphabetically)

Anshudeep Sharda

Apoorva Jha

Arvind Agnihotri

Dinesh Sharma

Kartika Nair

K P Vishwas

Kush Amin

Mansi Gohil

Mansi Mody

Mayank Agnihotri

Mridul Agnihotri

Neelam Sharma

Niyati Sharma

Ram Tirth Sharma

Shehban Patel

Shloka Bhuwalka

Shree Swamiji

Simran Sardana

Stuti Agnihotri

Vidhi Sharma

Vivek Nathaani

Vrushti Pancholi

the first readers said...

Hello from the You Own The Words! We are a writing community and event organizers based all over India regularly engaging in creative writing, projects, postings for our page and commercial writing.

Stuti Agnihotri has been a vital nerve in the community ever since its inception.

Her writings on our official Instagram handle are one of the most liked. In short, Stuti is a power house of words, activity and ideas.

Vishwas KP

Founder of the writing community
You Own The Words: Where Ink Flows in a Million Colours

Stuti's poems are emotional and enjoyable. Her poems decorated with poetic devices indicate a fantastic shift in valuation of poetry. Stuti spots beauty and interest in fragile feelings and portrays the truth through her poems. I bless her for her future endeavors. May her poems be the world in which the readers live and seek out things which resonate with them.

Manisha Vaishnav

English Teacher at The Aditya Birla School

It's short, sweet & simple. It connects with people's experiences! Keep up the good work.

Stuti Changle

Author & Entrepreneur - On The Open Road

Your Experiences

www.ingramcontent.com/pod-product-compliance
Lightning Source LLC
Chambersburg PA
CBHW051824130726
47987CB00003B/1398